Here's a story to share!

Sharing a story with your child is great fun and it's an ideal way to start your child reading.

The left-hand pages are 'your' story pages. The right-hand pages are specially written for your child with simple vocabulary and helpful repetition.

• Cuddle up close and look through the book together. What's happening in the pictures?

• Read the whole story to your child, both your story pages and your child's. Tell your child what it says on his* story pages and point to the words as you say them.

• Now it's time to read the story again and see if your child would like to join in and read his story pages along with you. Don't worry about perfect reading – what matters at this stage is having fun.

• It's best to stop when your child wants to. You can pick up the book at any time and enjoy sharing the story all over again.

Here the child is referred to as 'he'. All Ladybird books are equally suitable for both boys and girls.

Edited by Lorraine Horsley and Caroline Rashleigh
Designed by Alison Guthrie, Lara Stapleton and Graeme Hole

A catalogue record for this book is available from the British Library

Published by Ladybird Books Ltd
27 Wrights Lane London W8 5TZ
A Penguin Company

2 4 6 8 10 9 7 5 3 1

© LADYBIRD BOOKS LTD MMI

LADYBIRD and the device of a Ladybird are trademarks of Ladybird Books Ltd

My
SuperDad

by Dick Crossley
illustrated by Anni Axworthy

My dad doesn't look that tough,
His muscles aren't that great.
He needs glasses to watch telly
And he's a little overweight.

But my dad has a secret,
That's as secret as can be.
And the only ones who know it
Are Baby Jack and me.

4

My dad.

5

If ever there's a problem,
Or there's something to be feared,
One minute Dad is dozing
And the next — he's disappeared!

He slips out to the tool shed
Where he bangs and clangs about.
And we all ask, "What's Dad doing?"
But then **someone else** steps out...

What's Dad doing?

JUST LOOK AT THAT!
IT'S SUPERDAD!

He's the fastest Dad there's been!
The greatest superhero
That the world has ever seen.

Just look at that!

No monster is too fierce for him,
No enemy too bad.
There's never been a problem
Too big for SuperDad.

When a hungry, roaring cheetah
Escaped from the Royal Zoo,
And chased the Queen, to eat her,
We thought, "What will Dad do?"

What will Dad do?

11

JUST LOOK AT THAT!
IT'S SUPERDAD!

He's the bravest anywhere!
He fixed the angry cheetah
With his icy Super-Stare.

The cheetah looked quite frightened
And ran shaking to its den.
And the Queen said, "He's the bravest!
SuperDad's saved us all again."

Just look at that!

Then in the World Cup Final
As the seconds ticked away,
All our team were injured,
And they called out, "Who will play?"

Who will play?

JUST LOOK AT THAT!
IT'S SUPERDAD!

Already in his kit.
And our superhero player
Was an instant sporting hit.

He quickly scored three stunning goals,

KERPOW!

KERTHWACK!

KERTHWUP!

The crowd said, "He's the greatest!
He's helped us win the cup."

Just look at that!

And when a giant space-rock
Was falling on our town,
And all the people, terrified,
Cried, "What will we do now?"

What will we do now?

JUST LOOK AT THAT!
IT'S SUPERDAD!

He's the strongest man around!
He calmly stood and waited
As the rock came rushing down.

And as the people panicked,
Thinking it would squash them flat,
He whacked it back to outer space
With a giant baseball bat.

Just look at that!

So if you're in an earthquake,
Or a whirlwind comes your way,
Or aliens land in your back yard
And take your Gran away...

Keep your head, don't panic!
Although things may look bad.
You're not alone, pick up the phone,
And call for SuperDad.

Call for SuperDad!

23

And once he's rid your town of crime,
Or saved the world once more,
He'll rush back to his tool shed
And quietly shut the door.

He'll quickly whip his cape off,
Put his Normal Dad clothes on.
And slip back to the TV
Before you even know he's gone.

It's Dad!

Now since Dad does his best to hide
The secret life he leads,
You may be wondering how I know
All about his super deeds.

The answer is quite simple —
I learned everything I know
From the greatest Superhero ever —
SuperDad told me so!

My SuperDad!

Turn off the TV, close the door, too.
Here's a story to share for just me and you...

Inky-pinky blot

Who is the inky-pinky blot in the dark, dark pond? He asks everyone who goes by, but no one ever seems to know...

Caterpillars can't fly!

A baby caterpillar dreams of flying high in the sky but all her friends just laugh. What is she to do?

By the light of the Moon

Charlie the zoo keeper has gone home and the zoo is quiet. Now it's time for the animals to dance by the light of the moon...

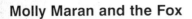

Molly Maran and the Fox

It's cold outside and Molly the kind-hearted hen says all the animals can stay in her warm barn. But how will she keep out the wily fox?